MW01146656

Ms. Magdalene's Halloween

Yvette Doolittle Herr

Yvette D. Herr

May an angel always be your guide.

Cover Design and Art
By
Linda Nichols

ISBN:
ISBN-13:978-1720607595

DEDICATION

To my husband, Travis.

ACKNOWLEDGMENTS

I give a heartfelt thank you to Linda Nichols, my husband's sister. Her artistic talent has always amazed me. Her spirit warms my heart, and her drawings vividly capture the mood of the story.

INTRODUCTION

Even when someone feels sad and lonely, there's still fun to be found, especially when a holiday like Halloween is just around the corner. All the saints come out on All Hallows Eve. The games are fun, and the candy is delightfully sweet, but no one can be certain how playful the saints will be on this one night.

Content

Ms. Magdalene's Halloween by Yvette Doolittle Herr

Chapter 1
A WEB OF MYSTERY

Ms. Magdalene was born in a house on Boggy Bayou, in Niceville, in the 1950s. The only child to arrive in the later years of her parents' lives was raised to be a very proper, charming, old-fashioned, southern girl. She received instructions on dressing appropriately for any social occasion and always acting politely, which was a requirement for her parents' parties at their house. It was an ideal setting for raising a happy, growing child.

It was a modest house, with just two bedrooms, but the vast yard and scenic Blue Water Bay surrounding it gave it a unique elegance. Cool evening breezes off the water and shade from the large hickory trees provided a perfect setting in the backyard.

1

People often gathered to be entertained and socialize.

Ms. Magdalene's father died when she was a young woman of twenty. She lived with and cared for her mother until she died a few years later. Afterward, Ms. Magdalene continued to live in the house on Boggy Bayou.

It wasn't long after her mother died that she married a man she'd known since she was a child. He and his younger brother lived in the house on the corner of the same street where she lived. Together, they owned and operated a shrimp boat.

Once again, the house on Boggy Bayou became the setting for fun-filled, social parties. Like her mother, Ms. Magdalene fashionably decorated her parties for any special occasion or holiday. She surrounded the hickory trees in the front yard with hundreds of bushes, and she landscaped the yard with flowers that bloomed in every season of the year.

After a few years of marriage and childlessness, Ms. Magdalene adopted a cat to keep her company while her husband, and his brother, spent many nights out in the bay catching shrimp. Soon after she acquired her cat, who she named Bandit, her husband tragically died in an accident on the shrimp boat. It happened to be on a rare night when his brother did not go with him. After the accident, the brother could never console Ms. Magdalene, and they rarely spoke to each other again.

The shock of losing her husband turned Ms. Magdalene into a more private person, almost a recluse. She often stayed alone at her house for days and weeks. Occasionally she hosted a party for a special event or holiday, but she mostly kept to herself.

She also seemed to be obsessed with being outside in her yard. The neighbors would watch as Ms. Magdalene wandered through the shrubbery with her cat Bandit, weaving through her legs and around her feet. Often they would see her with garden flowers in hand, Bandit following her, walking the two blocks from the house to the old city cemetery, where her family was buried. They believed her habit of visiting the cemetery to leave flowers from her yard at the graves of her loved ones was Ms. Magdalene's way to deal with her loss.

More recently, though, her yard started to look like a jungle, as she paid less and less attention to it.

Privately, though raised to be a very proper lady, Ms. Magdalene had kept one very improper habit a secret all of her life. It began in her childhood. She was out of control whenever she saw a spider hanging by a thread from its web.

The spiders were everywhere in the trees and bushes, in the yard. The first time she was overcome by her obsession, she stared at the red spider for hours, fascinated by the

4

iridescent spots on its back. She impulsively plucked it away from its home in the web, using her thumb and forefinger. She deposited the spider in a glass jar, leaving the spider's web to sway in the wind.

Soon, she became quick, plucking away many spiders from their web on any day she was free to be outside. She collected all the spiders in a glass jelly jar and took them to the attic in her house, where she released them.

The captured spiders were the size, and color, of a small red grape. The iridescent spots on their backs shone during the day and at night. Even though their natural home was in the trees and bushes, they quickly built new spiral webs on the walls, ceiling, and across the wood rafter beams once they were released into the attic.

For years, as a child, she would sneak up to the attic. Even as an adult, Ms. Magdalene often visited her attic, watching the spiders

5

work and inspecting their webs. The artwork in the spiders' webs excited and pleased her.

After her husband died, there were many days when she never left the attic. She sat there, with the spiders and Bandit too. When the evening turned into night, she would turn on the dim attic light and sit for hours before it was finally time to go to bed.

Ms. Magdalene died under strange circumstances, so some people thought. One day her neighbor, Sidney, saw her lying in the front yard beneath a large hickory tree. The doctors did not fully understand the symptoms of her illness when she arrived at the hospital. She was vomiting, delirious with fever, and had hundreds of purple blisters all over her body. Ms. Magdalene died in the hospital two days later.

At her funeral, people remembered the tremendous fun parties Ms. Magdalene had hosted. Still, they also talked about how she became so private in the last few years of her life. They wondered why the yard was so overgrown with bushes and why she allowed the branches of the hickory tree to grow over the top of the roof. Mostly they wondered about the light in the attic being on late into the night.

Ms. Magdalene's husband's younger brother, who still lived in the house at the end of her street, inherited Ms. Magdalene's house. He decided to rent it and made arrangements to have it cleaned. That was when Ms. Magdalene's lifelong obsession was discovered.

The house cleaners found a small wood stool placed directly beneath a bare lightbulb hanging from the center attic beam. Around the beam and chair were hundreds of dusty, glass, jelly jars; thousands of spiders; and millions of cobwebs.

Chapter 2
HOLLIE AND COOKIES

Hollie felt sad and lonely when she was forced to move into the old house on Boggy Bayou in Niceville. She was eleven and an only child. She missed the friends she grew up with living in Panama City. A lot!

Although the town's name had a pleasant sound, there hadn't been any lovely memories for Hollie since the beginning of the summer. Which was when they moved into the house after her parents found new jobs.

When she started school, Hollie thought she would quickly make new friends, but everyone seemed different. She'd met new people in her new school. They were polite, but it was not the same as going to school with the friends she left behind. The new students did not know anything about Hollie as her old friends did.

The new classmates did not know about the time Hollie sang and danced in the fourth-grade school play. Or, when in the third grade, she made a funny poster display of different amphibians for her entry in the science fair, and everyone laughed at the comments she wrote beneath the pictures. Or, when in the fifth grade, she won an award for the highest ticket sales in her elementary school fundraiser for playground renovations.

Everyone seemed to be only interested in talking about the things they had done over the summer or what happened in school last year. Hollie didn't know where or how to start making new friends at her new school in Niceville.

It was good that Hollie had one good friend who she could talk to. Her cat was her best friend now.

Cookies was a short-haired, solid-black female with long, black whiskers and a long, thin tail that she held up straight whenever she followed Hollie around the house. Her eyes were bright, glossy green.

When Hollie got home from school each day, she was alone until her mother arrived after five o'clock, tired from a busy day at her new job.

It was a warm, beautiful fall day in October. Still, it had been another horrible, terrible, awful day at school for Hollie.

The first thing Hollie did when she got inside the house was to pick up Cookies, who always jumped from Hollie's bedroom window, and waited at the front door for Hollie when she heard the school bus stop on the road. Hollie carried both Cookies and her backpack to her bedroom.

Hollie dropped the backpack on the floor, flopped on her back on the bed with Cookies in her arms, and gave Cookies a big bundle of hugs.

"Oh, Cookies," Hollie moaned. "If it wasn't for you, I. . . ." Hollie stopped in the middle of her sentence. She tasted salt on her tongue and tried hard to prevent the tears from coming but choked on a sob. She didn't want to cry again in front of Cookies, as she had been doing so often lately.

"I just hate it here. If it wasn't for you, I don't think I could make it through every day. I only look forward to coming home and seeing you!"

Cookies purred and licked the salty tears off of Hollie's nose.

"The people at school are nice, but they seem so different from my old friends. They don't know me. They laugh at things that don't seem funny to me. Sometimes I feel like they are talking about me when they laugh. I don't know why!" Hollie bemoaned. "It seems so pointless to talk to people who don't seem interested in what you have to say."

Cookies meowed several times like she was trying to say something to make Hollie feel better. Then Cookies rubbed her head against Hollie's face and purred into her ear.

Like magic, Cookies had a way of turning Hollie's day into a happy one after she got home from school. Hollie felt the lump in her throat shrink and the heaviness in her heart become lighter.

"Why do I, we, have to be living in Niceville, Cookies?"

Lying on the bed, staring up at the ceiling, Hollie remembered how the morning began.

For a week, Hollie had been waking up early every morning, when it was still dark and before it was time to get up and get ready for school. Something woke her up, but what? Each time it happened, in drowsy confusion, she would look at the clock and ask herself, "Where am I?"

When she realized where she was, she was heartbroken.

Hollie rolled over to her side and snuggled Cookies in her arms.

"We've lived here for five months now," she said to Cookies. "Everything about living here, in this house, feels wrong. Anyway, let's go to the kitchen. I'm hungry. I'm going to fix something to eat."

Chapter 3
THE HOUSE ON BOGGY BAYOU

Hollie got up and walked out of her bedroom, down the hall, to the kitchen.

Cookies jumped off the bed and followed Hollie. Her paws padded down the carpeted hallway.

Cookies was an intelligent cat and knew the word kitchen. It usually meant a cat treat. Cookies loved to eat just about anything, even peanut butter.

On the day Cookies was brought home as a kitten, she was starving. Hollie had carried her into the house and placed her down on the kitchen floor to explore her new surroundings. The first thing Cookies did was sniff out a chunk of sugar cookie lying beneath the kitchen table. Despite being stressed from riding in a car, Cookies found the piece of cookie and licked it up off the floor. The crunching sound made by her small, sharp teeth caused Hollie and her mom to laugh and shout out in unison, cookies.

"We can call her Sugar Cookies," Hollie's mom suggested, but Hollie decided that just Cookies would be a cute name for her cat.

Adjusting to Niceville was not as hard for Cookies as it had been for Hollie. The house smelled old, which made it more interesting, and the window views outside entertained her when she was home alone.

The bay window in Hollie's bedroom was Cookie's favorite place to sit. A tall, hickory tree with long, thick, crooked branches reached out wide and above the house's roof. Some of the large branches even touched the roof. Over one hundred azalea bushes and other wildflowers covered the front yard. From the cozy nook in Hollie's bedroom window, Cookies could watch birds, squirrels, and spiders.

Cookies sat in the window all day until the school bus stopped in front of the house to drop off Hollie. Cookies watched until Hollie stepped off the bus. Then, Cookies raced to the side window at the front door to watch Hollie walk down the driveway to the house.

Hollie's parents' bedroom also had a bay window, but the view was much different. It faced the backyard of the house, which bordered the open waters of Blue Water Bay.

The two-hundred-foot-long yard, also covered with many bushes and trees, was surrounded by a chain-link fence. A gate in the fence opened to a long, wood dock that stretched a hundred feet into the water. Sometimes seagulls flying across the bay landed on the dock, but it was too far away for Cookies to get a good look at them. There was much more entertaining activity in the front yard tree.

"No treats for you today Cookies, I'm afraid," Hollie said to Cookies in a serious voice when they got to the kitchen. "Mom says you're getting too fat. We need to put you on a diet."

Cookies flopped down on her side on the cool, tile kitchen floor and watched every move Hollie made. Despite what Hollie said, if Cookies was lucky, she still might get a small tidbit of Hollie's sandwich.

The house was quiet while Hollie prepared herself a peanut butter and jelly sandwich.

Hollie placed her sandwich on a paper napkin. She carried a glass of milk in one hand and the sandwich in the other.

Cookies followed Hollie through the living room to a door that opened into a glass-enclosed patio. Hollie took a step down into the patio, careful not to spill the milk. She rounded a corner-brick wall and entered a small, closet-sized space that her dad used as an office. The office had a window-sized opening in the wall adjoining the living room.

Hollie felt comfortable being alone at home in the office. It allowed her to see the living room front door and a view of the backyard through the glass-enclosed patio and Blue Water Bay.

Cookies jumped to the top of the office desk and sat in front of Hollie.

"Now you lie down and be good," Hollie instructed Cookies. She put her glass of milk and sandwich down on the desk. Cookies purred when Hollie patted her on the head.

"Mom said that I could invite some of my old friends over for a weekend sleep-over. She said they'd love to come over here because we could play in the big backyard and go in the water. I'd much rather go to Panama City to spend a weekend over there. I'd see a lot more of my old friends again."

Hollie took a big bite and munched down on her sandwich. She swallowed her food and gulped her milk.

"I don't know. Maybe mom is right. I know Cherie and Allie would wonder about living in an old house like this one. They'd explore it and ask questions about all the curious features. The kitchen cabinets are old and stained. The floor carpet is worn out. This glass-enclosed patio, with a hot tub inside it, is different. Who thought of putting a hot tub in a glass patio? This little office is kind of weird, too.

"Cherie and Allie would definitely like the deck and big backyard. I'm sure they've never seen a tree, like the one here, growing right in the middle of the deck.

"They'd probably like walking out on the dock, but I don't think they'd like to go in the water. It's not like swimming in the Gulf of Mexico, with clear, blue water and white sand. The water in the bay is clear, but the sand is yucky, brown. Too bad we don't have a boat."

Hollie briefly stopped talking to take another bite of her sandwich. Cookies waited patiently for a treat.

"Mom said she saw dolphins in the water out at the end of the dock. I didn't tell mom or dad, but I could swear to you, Cookies, that one morning I saw the back of a huge alligator. It was swimming in the water, close to the shoreline, and went underneath the dock. That's another good reason not to go in the water here."

Cookies stared at Hollie while she talked. She would wait for Hollie to finish eating her sandwich before she jumped off the desk to grab a few nibbles of her cat food from her bowl in the laundry room.

Hollie continued to tell Cookies her ideas. "Anyway, I know Cherie won't like the tiny bathroom I have to use. The skylight above the bathtub is unusual because you can see the tree's limbs outside above the roof. Still, there's barely enough room to turn around in the bathroom. It always has a dank, musty, smell too. Cherie wouldn't like that.

"Allie would probably like the window seat in my bedroom. I think mom and dad's bedroom window seat better. Daylight comes into their room from their window. The view of the bay is pretty, too. My bedroom is always dark. It's because all the branches from the tree in the front yard block out all the sunlight. That's one of the reasons why I like to leave my blinds closed. Why bother keeping them open if the tree doesn't let in any light?

"But, the biggest reason for keeping the blinds closed is because my window faces the road. The street light shines through the tree limbs and casts dark, weird-shaped shadows across the yard at night. It's creepy. It makes me think that something is out there trying to look into my window. Maybe that's why I wake up early."

Hollie closed her eyes and shook her head to get the thought out of her mind. When she opened her eyes, she put her face close to Cookie's face to be sure she was listening. "You know what I think Cherie and Allie would really like, Cookies?"

Cookies blinked both eyes and meowed as if to ask Hollie what.

"They'd love to walk through the cemetery that's up the street. Yes, I think my friends would find walking through an old cemetery exciting. It's so close to Halloween. We could pretend that there are ghosts in the cemetery. I bet Cherie and Allie have never walked through a cemetery before."

Cookies sensed the excitement in Hollie's voice. She twitched her ears, sat up, and stretched out her front paws to get ready to jump to the floor.

"When I walked through the cemetery with mom last week, something made the hair on my arms and legs tingle. I thought it must be a breeze from the bay, but it still felt strange. I felt like someone was watching me."

Cookies blinked her eyes as if to agree.

"I think it must be a haunted cemetery!" Hollie said very seriously.

Hollie picked up her empty glass and stood up to leave the office.

Cookies jumped off the desk to follow Hollie back to the kitchen. She darted past Hollie's feet and skidded across the kitchen's tile floor. She paced in circles around Hollie's legs, still hoping for a treat.

Hollie plopped her glass and crumpled napkin on the counter and ignored Cookies' begging, turned around, and returned to her bedroom.

Chapter 4
THE OLD CEMETERY

Hollie's bedroom window blinds were closed, making her feel safe when she was alone in the house. Occasionally her mom opened them in the morning before they left together for the ride to school, where her mom dropped her off before going to work.

Hollie watched TV for an hour every day before she started to work on her homework. She had to finish her homework before her mom came home from work. That was a rule.

Hollie turned on her small TV to her favorite cartoon channel. She laid down in bed on her stomach with her arms folded over a pillow and her chin cupped by her hands.

Hollie could hear Cookies crunching on her dry cat food in the laundry room next to the

25

kitchen and the garage. Minutes later, Cookies jumped on Hollie's bed.

Hollie missed being able to participate in after-school activities. In her old school, she'd taken art classes, dancing, and gymnastics. That's where she met her best friends, Cherie and Allie. Hollie's Mom had promised she could take up an after-school activity again once she finished her first year of school in Niceville.

It was a long time to wait. Each day and week seemed to go a little faster now that she was back in school, but she'd have to get through another summer. It seemed to take forever for last summer to end.

Hollie found herself not paying any attention to the cartoons on TV. They didn't distract her from thinking about the things that were worrying her.

She rolled over to her back, folded her hands behind her head, and stared up at the ceiling.

"Mom and Dad don't understand how bad I feel about living here," she moaned to Cookies. "I can't talk to them about anything anymore. They're always tired when they come home from work. Sixth grade is hard enough without worrying about having friends and fun. I'm tired of being lonely.

 "Last summer, I talked to Cherie and Allie on the phone all the time. Since school started, they don't call me very often. They'll come here, but that will only be for a couple of days. I love you, Cookies, but you can't talk to me. "

Taking them to the cemetery reminded Hollie how angry she became with her mother after visiting the cemetery last Saturday. She began to think, again, about her plans for Cherie and Allie's visit. Something her mother said was still bothering her.

Hollie recalled that day.

The cemetery was only two blocks away from Hollie's house. It was an old, small, city cemetery that covered an entire block of the neighborhood. It held some of the city's original pioneer families.

Concrete stones marked the graves of people from infants to the very old. They were worn down from weather and time. Black mold filled the inscriptions, which had the person's name, date of birth, and date of death.

"It's too hot to be walking around here," Hollie complained, stomping her feet through the entrance gate of the cemetery, kicking up sand and dust. "There's not even a tree to give us shade from the sun."

"Hollie, we're probably only going to spend fifteen minutes here," her mom said, adding in her annoying, let's always try to be cheerful voice, "We might find something interesting."

"Like what?" Hollie asked sarcastically, not at all interested in walking around a cemetery or hearing an answer to the question.

"Well, for example, the names of people are different from common names we hear today. We can read from the dates how old they lived to be. Sometimes we can see what kind of work they did by the shapes of the monuments," and she pointed to a tall monument shaped like a log. "That person probably worked as a logger or tree cutter. We can also see how many people from the same family were buried together. We can read the kind thoughts of people who loved them wrote about them. Look!" Hollie's mom became excited. "Here's a group of markers all with the same family name. There are men, women, children, and grandparents."

Hollie's mom walked alone, stopping at several concrete grave markers to read the inscriptions. Hollie lingered at a family plot.

29

She didn't read anything and kept her eyes focused on where her mom walked next. Hollie hoped it would be back to the cemetery entrance gate.

Hollie's mom reached a stone marker that stood out amongst the rest. "Hollie, come over here. Look at this one."

Hollie's mom was standing outside a boundary of small limestone, rocks set around a tall, oval-shaped, pink, marble gravestone.

Hollie sauntered toward her mother, who had already started to talk fast, as she often did when excited.

"We can figure out from the dates and names, on the left side of the stone, that these people are probably the parents of the woman named Magdalene, whose name is on the right side. Magdalene has two last names, one of which is the same as the other two people. It looks like Magdalene, and her husband, are buried with her parents.

"What's interesting about this gravestone is

the color of the marble. I don't think I've ever seen a pink marble gravestone quite this dark. The color is almost red. The white veins in the marble have a beautiful lace pattern. I can't imagine where they found this marble. And, over here, to the side, there's a small black stone in the ground with the single name Bandit on it. I wonder if that was a pet. It must have been a pet, but it doesn't say. There's not a date on it, either."

Hollie was not at all interested in connecting the names of dead people. "I don't need to know who died and when they died. What I'd like to know more about is how they used to dress and the clothes they wore back then," she said to her mother.

"Listen to me, Hollie," her mother snapped in irritation. "Who you are, or who you will become in life, is not always going to be about what you wear. Other things matter."

Hollie's mom paused to take a deep breath

then said, "It's not just about what you wear or how you look. The beauty that lives on the inside of a person is much more important than the beauty we look for on the outside. It's the deeds that matter. People who have been here before us are a part of our life, too, because of the things they did to shape the course of our history."

Hollie had heard these words from her mother more than once. Hollie knew she was better off not to say anything about what she thought or how she felt to her mom. Her mom didn't seem to care about what was essential to Hollie.

"I only want to be myself," Hollie angrily thought, "not what someone else thinks I should be."

Hollie's mom resumed walking further into the cemetery. "Come look at this!" she called out to Hollie, again excited, like a person who had just found money.

Hollie dragged her feet over to where her mom stood. "What?!" she asked stubbornly.

Her mom was staring down at a small square stone, the size of a brick, barely visible above the dirt.

"Look there," Hollie's mom pointed down.

Inscribed on the stone were the words Civil War Veteran.

"This means this cemetery has been here since the Civil War, or maybe longer. I didn't know that the city of Niceville was this old. The cemetery has been here since the 1800s."

"Uh, huh," Hollie grunted, unimpressed and not interested.

"I'd hope you might find this small gravestone a little bit interesting. Just think,

Hollie. There were soldiers from this part of Florida fighting in the Civil War. If you want to think about clothes, imagine the uniforms those men had to wear in this kind of heat. This cemetery is quite historical!" Hollie's mom exclaimed.

Hollie gave a pleading can we go now look at her mom.

"Okay, it's too hot and I can tell you're not very interested. Maybe we should come up here and walk around at night. There might be ghosts flying around. You might find it more exciting then." Hollie's mom laughed.

"Geeze, mom, we live two blocks away from a cemetery, and you have to tell me that dead people in this cemetery can come out at night as ghosts!" Hollie said, angry at her mom for saying something she didn't want to hear.

"Take it easy, Hollie. You don't have to worry about ghosts," her mom laughed again. "They are not real"!

Chapter 5
THE NIGHTMARE

Since visiting the cemetery, Hollie hadn't stopped thinking about it. She didn't know why, but she felt a strong urge to return to it. She hoped going back with Cherie and Allie would be a better experience and change her feelings about it.

"All right, Cookies, it's time to turn off the TV and do my homework. It's all due tomorrow. Thankfully, tomorrow is Friday. I'll have all weekend and won't have to do homework."

After dinner, the family watched one TV program together, then fell into bed.

Hollie had the cemetery visit on her mind and was unable to sleep. She thought about the dead people in the ground, so close to her bedroom. She wished her mom had never said anything about ghosts last Saturday.

The streetlight shone through the tiny, cracked openings in the closed blinds. With Cookies snuggled up against her legs, Hollie felt somewhat safe. And, after all, her parents were in their bedroom across the hall. She should feel safe, but she found herself shaking and afraid. Hollie's eyes searched in the dark for anything that might move. She listened for any strange noise. Her eyes searched the room for any moving, shadowy object.

"What's that!!?!" She trembled.

"Eyes! It's a pair of blue eyes above the TV on the dresser. They're moving! No, they're floating. It can't be real, but I see them. Yes, there are two blue eyes!" Hollie pulled up the covers to touch her nose.

Two blue orbs, the size of marbles, glowed in the dark. They floated above the dresser.

They shone, twinkled, blinked, and seemed to stare directly at Hollie. There was no head, no face, no mouth, no nose.

Hollie's legs trembled, which stirred Cookies to wake up. Cookies opened her eyes, yawned, and turned her head toward Hollie as if to ask what's wrong?

"Look, Cookies. Look at the wall over there. Do you see those eyes?" Hollie whispered, trying to stay calm.

She took Cookie's head in both of her hands and turned it to face the wall. Hollie felt Cookie's body grow stiff and heard her growl.

Cookies leaped off the bed and ran into the hallway. The orbs suddenly disappeared.

"Cookies! Cookies!" Hollie whispered, more loudly, anxious for her to return. She shifted her eyes from the wall to the doorway, then back to the wall. "Cookies, come back!"

Hollie waited, trembling until Cookies jumped back onto the bed. Hollie grabbed Cookie's body and held her close to her face.

Cookies snuggled her head into Hollie's shoulder.

The remainder of the night was primarily sleepless for Hollie.

Just before daylight, Hollie woke up from a horrible dream.

"I hate you! Go away; I hate you!" She screamed, bolted up in bed, and rubbed her eyes. When she was able to open them, she saw a dark shadow floating in the room, near the window.

Afraid, Hollie tried to determine if the formless, shifting, blobby, dark shadow in the grey light was real. The dark shadow quickly disappeared.

Hollie thought, "Maybe it's hiding beneath my bed or in the closet."

Hollie tried to control her fear. "I know it was a dream, but it felt so real."

Hollie felt the bed move. Something had to be lying on the floor beneath her bed. Did she hear a noise too, or was it her imagination?

Hollie soon realized that her legs, stretched out in front of her, was shaking, and bouncing uncontrollably. She swallowed hard to catch her breath.

Cookies sat up, yawned, and stretched.

"Without you, Cookies, how could I get through the night?" she said near tears. "It is Friday. Thank goodness it's not Friday the thirteenth!"

Hollie didn't need an alarm to wake her up for school. After her dream, she lay in bed, waiting for full daylight, which didn't come soon enough on this October morning.

When she got home from school, a very tired Hollie retreated to the back of the house to sit outside on the wood deck. She felt safer sitting outside rather than watching TV in her scary bedroom.

The nightmare had bothered her all day, but there was no one at school or at home that she could talk to about it.

Hollie sat on the metal glider. Cookies lay on the deck next to Hollie's feet, with her leash securely tied to the chair. Hollie stared out over the bay, looking for birds, boats, or anything to distract her and keep her from thinking about last night.

When her mom arrived home, she was surprised to find Hollie sitting outside. "Well, it's good to see you getting out of the house. It's a nice, cool night to sit outside," she said to Hollie. "I'm going in the kitchen to get snacks and supper ready. Your dad will be home soon."

As much as she tried, Hollie couldn't stop thinking about the things she saw in her bedroom.

"It was a pretty scary night last night, wasn't it Cookies? First, we see blue eyes floating above the TV. I know a dream woke me up, but I can't remember what it was about. After I woke up, I'm sure that I saw a shadow, or blob, move above me and across the room. I know I saw it!"

Chapter 6
RED EYES AT NIGHT

It was a Friday night routine. Hollie, her parents, and Cookies sat on the back deck to unwind and relax after a busy week at work and school.

The late October early evening sky was clear, turning into blended orange, pink, and lavender shades on the horizon. Just before the sun settled below the last line of blue, its bright rays shone through glittering strings of spider webs hanging from the trees and the tall coastal reeds growing in the bayou water.

"How was school today, Hollie?"

Hollie heard the cheery voice of her father when he opened the back door of the patio. He stepped out and walked across the wood

43

deck to nestle beside Hollie on the glider. He patted Hollie on the shoulder and reached down to pat Cookies on the head. His warm greeting calmed Hollie. Her stomach had been turning flip-flops all day.

"Fine," Hollie answered.

"Anything new going on?" he asked.

"Nope," she said. "Hey, look at all those spider webs over there." Hollie quickly pointed in the direction of the coastal reeds and setting sun. A gentle breeze blew through the reeds. "Isn't that cool looking?" she asked her dad.

"Yes. Yes, it is, for sure," he replied.

They were quiet for a few minutes, admiring the spectacle of thousands of silky spider webs swaying and floating in midair, glittering in the last rays of the sun.

"Think about how many spiders it took to create all of that!" her dad spoke first.

"I don't want to think about the spiders," Hollie playfully shrieked. "It's those webs that are beautiful. Remember that big spider we saw hanging from the big tree in the front yard?"

"You're right. Seriously, I wouldn't want to see a spider that big inside the house," he said. "Hey, look out there. There goes the shrimper."

Hollie's dad pointed his finger out to the bay.

The shrimp boat was a beautiful sight to see, with its colored lights and its nets opened out wide, ready to scoop up shrimp swimming in the bay.

"I wonder if he stays out all night," Hollie asked.

"Probably," her dad answered.

"Here's snacks and drinks," the sing-song voice of Hollie's mom interrupted their conversation. She shoved the porch door open with her shoulder and stepped onto the deck carrying a tray loaded with small plates, snacks, drinks, and napkins. "Did I overhear you guys talking about shrimp? Well, guess what we have for a snack tonight? Boiled shrimp."

Hollie's mom set the tray down on a small table, and they began to peel the shrimp.

Cookies sat up and sniffed the air, hoping for a treat.

While they ate, Hollie's mom talked.

"I was talking to the lady next door the other night before you came home," she said. "I can't remember her name right now, though. She was telling me about the woman who originally owned this house. Her parents bought the land in the 1950s and had the house built. Her dad died when she was young. She stayed with her mother in the house until her mother died. When she married, she and her husband stayed in the

46

house. Her husband was a shrimper who owned his boat. He died in a boating accident. She never remarried and lived here alone. After she died four years ago, the family decided to rent this house. The man who lives in the house at the end of this street, down on the corner, is the husband's brother. He's the one who owns the shrimp boat out there and this house."

"Well, you're just full of all kinds of news tonight," Hollie's dad joked.

Hollie's mom ignored his comment and continued to talk while eating. "I find it surprising that someone has lived in a house all of their life. You don't hear that anymore. There's a lot of history in this house. The neighbor said we're the second family to rent the house. The first renters, an elderly couple, needed the dock for their boat but moved after they sold the boat."

"Did the neighbor tell you if the brother-in-law down the street is interested in selling the house?" Hollie's dad asked. "The real estate company we used to find a rental house didn't mention that the owner lives on the same street. It seems strange that he wouldn't introduce himself to us."

"No, she didn't say anything about the house being for sale," Hollie's mom answered.

She thought for a moment. "Oh, now I remember the neighbor's name. Her name is Sidney. Her husband, Mike, is not in good health," Hollie's mom seemed relieved to remember the names of the neighbors. "She mentioned the name of the woman who lived in this house, but I can't remember right now. She said they were good friends, and she still misses her."

"I wonder why the brother-in-law didn't move into this house after he inherited it." Hollie's dad said. "That puzzles me. I think this is a nicer house than the one on the corner."

"Maybe he doesn't like this house. He might think it's haunted," Hollie said.

Hollie's parents' eyes locked. They were puzzled and concerned, hearing Hollie's strange comment. Neither knew what to say.

Hollie's mom abruptly rose from her seat.

"So, I think it's time to go inside and finish cooking our dinner," Hollie's mom said.

"I'll help," Hollie's dad said, rising to follow her.

"I'm staying outside until dinner is ready," Hollie said. "The breezes out here are nice."

The lights of the shrimp boat grew smaller as it slipped further out into the bay. The sky had turned a dark grey. A thick autumn fog began to rise above the surface of the water.

Cookies remained with Hollie, lying on the deck by her feet.

"Come and sit up here with me, Cookies," Hollie said and patted on the glider where her dad had been sitting.

She didn't mind sitting outside in the dark with Cookies sitting near her on the glider. She knew her parents were nearby, in the kitchen. More importantly, she wanted to avoid her bedroom; as much as possible.

Hollie rocked the glider. She squinted, focusing her eyes on the twinkling lights from the windows of tall condominium buildings across the bay, four miles away.

Something else caught her attention. She tried to identify what she was seeing. Two bright, red eyes hovered above the water at the front of the dock. It was hard to know how large they were. It was so far away, yet seemed close. At first, Hollie thought there must be a body attached to the eyes.

"What body, or animal, has red eyes?" she thought. "Are those things moving?"

50

She sat at the edge of the glider, hoping to bring the objects closer into view.

"Yes, I see them moving." Hollie panicked. "They're moving away from the dock and coming closer into the yard!"

Hollie reached over to pick up Cookies lying next to her on the glider. Her fur was fluffed out. She growled and fixed her eyes on the yard.

"You see it too, don't you? I'm scared, Cookies! Last night we saw blue eyes floating above my TV in my bedroom. Tonight we see red eyes floating by the dock. What can those be? Let's go inside now!"

Hollie untied the leash, grabbed Cookies, and stumbled over the step from the deck into the patio. Her heart was racing. She was out of breath when she got inside the house carrying Cookies.

Her parents did not notice that anything was wrong.

Chapter 7
BLUE EYES RETURN

After dinner, Hollie and her parents settled into the living room. They stretched out on the sofa recliner to watch a movie on TV. Cookies nestled in between their legs. It was another Friday night routine.

Typically, both parents were asleep before the movie ended. Hollie would sometimes wake them up, but tonight she lingered on the sofa long after the movie ended. She listened to their heavy, rhythmic breathing. Her dad began to snore louder.

"I have no idea what they were. What if those red eyes we saw outside find a way into the house tonight and show up in my bedroom?" Hollie fearfully thought.

She whispered, "I'm afraid, Cookies. I don't like to be alone in my bedroom, even if you're with me in bed."

Hollie knew that eventually, her parents would wake up by themselves, as they often did when the room got quiet after a movie ended.

Hollie's dad was the first to stir. "Well, okay then," he said and gently nudged Hollie's mom with his foot. "Looks like your mother missed another ending of a movie."

"I think I heard you snore first," Hollie said, defending her mother.

Hollie's mother groaned. Using both hands, she pushed her tired body off the couch.

"Time to call it a night and shut off all the lights," Hollie's dad announced.

"Oh, I wish I didn't have to," Hollie thought.

Defiantly she said, "I'll get to bed. Don't worry."

"Something wrong, Hollie?" her dad asked, suddenly surprised at her tone. It wasn't the way the daughter he loved usually talked to him.

"No." she quickly answered.

"Okay. Then we'll see you in the morning. Tomorrow is Saturday, and we all get to sleep late. Good night, Hollie," he said.

Her parents went into their bedroom and shut the door.

Hollie went into her bedroom and left her door open. Hollie thought she heard a softer voice echo her dad's.

Good night.

Hollie shook her head. It had to be her mother saying *goodnight* to her.

"It won't be a good night," she muttered.

Cookies lagged behind. Crouching low on all four paws, the cat slowly and quietly crept down the hallway. When she reached the open bedroom door, she stopped.

Hollie patted her bed. It was her signal to Cookies to get up on the bed. "C'mon Cookies," she urged her cat. "Hurry up."

Cookies sat on her haunches. She was staring at the closed closet door at the end of the hallway with her head cocked to the side, ears perked up, whiskers twitching, and eyes opened wide again.

It was a storage closet, used for linens and some unpacked boxes, between both bedrooms.

Hollie hissed a whisper, "What are you waiting for?"

She tip-toed two steps toward Cookies. Holding onto her bedroom door handle, Hollie turned her head to look down the hall, back toward the living room. "There's nothing in there!" Hollie whispered a little louder, becoming irritated and impatient, with Cookies.

Suddenly Cookies reared up on her two hind legs and pawed at the closet door with her two front paws. It looked like she was trying to dig a hole through the wood. Her paws moved fast. Up and down. Up and down. She sat back down for a moment. She stretched her body and started up again. Her paws clawed against the wood door, making a loud noise.

"What's going on out there?" Hollie's dad called out from behind his closed bedroom door.

Hollie, startled, stared at Cookies and said, "I have no idea!"

Her dad slid off his bed, opened his bedroom door, and stepped into the hallway.

"What the heck are you up to?" He was asking both Hollie and Cookies. He watched

Cookies continue to paw at the closet door for a minute. Then he quickly opened it.

Hollie, taken by surprise, stumbled backward.

On the other hand, cookies jumped inside the closet on the top of an unopened box sitting on the floor. From the box, she bounded up to the first shelf. Cookies began to paw through the towels stored on the shelf.

"Good grief. This cat is acting like an idiot," Hollie's dad laughed and watched Cookies paw at the linens like a maniac. "She's probably heard a bug or something small crawling around. This house needs a lot of cleaning. All of these trees and bushes around here don't help with the problem of critters. Don't worry, Hollie. Tomorrow I'll do some spraying for whatever might be roaming around inside and outside," he said and yawned. "Now, let's go to bed and get some rest. Get Cookies and keep your door shut, so she doesn't get back out in the hall and try to dig a hole through the door, okay?"

"Not okay," Hollie thought. Closing her bedroom door was the last thing Hollie wanted to do, but she couldn't tell her dad the reason why.

Hollie raised her eyes and pulled on Cookies, who still had her claws dug deep into the linens. Hollie dragged Cookies off the shelf and carried her into her bedroom.

"I've got a flashlight somewhere in this mess," she said, after shutting her bedroom door and tossing Cookies onto the bed.

Hollie found her small flashlight in a drawer. She turned it on before she turned off the ceiling light.

Hollie held the flashlight tightly while she lay beneath her bed covers. The tiny bulb of the flashlight cast a light bright enough for Hollie to see a glow above the covers.

Once her eyes adjusted to the dim light in the dark room, she felt her skin tingle. Her arms and legs began to shake.

Cookies sat rigidly by Hollie's side, with her head and ears perked high.

A pair of blue eyes appeared above the TV. Like the night before, the eyes glowed, blinked, and floated, moving from one side of the TV to the other.

Cookies and Hollie watched the eyes for hours until their own eyes fluttered shut from exhaustion.

The next day, and Sunday, Hollie wanted to stay out of her bedroom as much as possible. She helped her dad spray for bugs and helped her mom cook and clean. She tried to do anything but spend time in her bedroom and dreaded when it became time to go to bed.

The blue eyes made appearances on Saturday night and Sunday night. It was no different than Friday night.

Throughout the weekend, Hollie could not tell her parents what she saw. How would they believe her story? They never even asked what she meant when she mentioned that the man down the street wouldn't want to live in a haunted house.

She couldn't talk to them about anything that was troubling her.

Chapter 8
KNOCKS IN THE ATTIC

Even after only a few hours of sleep, Hollie was awake before her alarm clock buzzed on Monday morning. She could hear the muffled voices of her mom and dad talking in the kitchen through her closed bedroom door.

"If only I could tell them what I've seen. If only Cookies could talk!" Hollie thought when she slid out of bed.

Hollie was eager to leave the house and wasted no time getting ready for school.

"You're out here early for a Monday morning," her dad said when she appeared in the kitchen, already dressed.

Cookies flopped down her fat, furry body and sprawled out in the middle of the floor. She was tired too. She looked up at Hollie, then turned her head toward Hollie's dad.

"I wish you wouldn't do that!" Hollie's mom scolded Cookies in a sharp voice. "One day, I'll either step on you or trip over you. One of us is going to get hurt!"

"You've always got to be the center of attention, don't you, Cookies?" Hollie's dad said playfully.

Hollie began to feel more relaxed. Soon she would be leaving the house. She had been so stressed since Friday night. The Monday morning routine felt normal compared to the last three nights. Today was the very first time she looked forward to going to the new school since the first day of sixth grade.

On top of missing her old friends, Hollie also found out that sixth grade was not so easy. As if making new friends wasn't challenging enough, she found herself struggling in her classes. English class, which had always been her favorite subject because she loved to read, was even hard. Her classes required a lot more work this year.

At the beginning of the school year, Hollie enjoyed having something to do after school besides watch TV. The homework helped to pass the time when she came home to the empty house. When the lesson became more difficult, Hollie would give up.

At the end of the day on Monday, the teacher returned the weekly homework assignments the students turned in on Friday.

Hollie sat at her desk watching the teacher, Ms. Smith, walk down the aisle between the desks as she handed out the homework that she had graded over the weekend. When she stopped at Hollie's desk, she touched Hollie lightly on the shoulder before placing the graded paper down.

"Hollie, you'll need to get your parents to sign this and bring it back to me tomorrow," she said in a soft, sympathetic voice.

"Yes, ma'am," Hollie said.

Hollie's trembling fingers held the paper. Her eyes became glued to the big red letter F at the top of the homework paper.

Hollie became overcome with a different feeling of fear. "I'm going to be in so much trouble when mom and dad see this," she thought.

When she got off the bus later that afternoon, Hollie raced to get inside the same house she was so anxious to leave in the morning. She wasn't thinking about the past three stressful nights, or Cherie and Allie coming for the weekend, or the creepy cemetery.

She dropped her book bag by the front door, ran past Cookies waiting at the door, flopped on top of her bed, and buried her face into her pillow. Hollie broke into sobs. A flood of tears that she'd struggled to hold back all day fell freely.

Cookies jumped up on the bed, and all she could do was watch and listen. Hollie wouldn't turn over and let her lick the tears off her cheeks.

An hour later, Hollie finally stopped crying.

"I have to think about my grades. Crying won't help," Hollie said to Cookies. "I'm sorry, Cookies. I'm not feeling like having a snack today."

Instead of turning on the TV, she worked on her homework in her dad's office, doing the best she could. By the time Hollie's parents both came home, she was composed. She'd washed her face several times to remove any hint of crying.

When everyone was finished eating dinner and it was time to clean up the plates, Hollie decided it was time to talk. She had been quiet ever since her parents came home, which wasn't unusual lately.

"Mom. Dad. Before we leave the table, I'd like to talk," she announced in an adult-like voice. "I've been thinking about something for a while, and I need to get it off my chest."

"Well, Hollie," her mom protested. "Can't this wait until after the dishes get put away?"

"I can do dishes," her dad spoke before Hollie had a chance to answer. "Let's just get them in the sink."

"Well, okay," Hollie's mom agreed without hesitating. She was curious about Hollie's sudden announcement.

"First, I have to get something out of my bedroom. I'll be right back." Hollie jumped out of her seat at the table and rushed down the hallway. She grabbed the homework papers she completed that afternoon and the homework papers that needed to be signed.

68

"Wonder what she's got up her sleeve?" Hollie's dad nudged at her mom as they carried dishes to the kitchen sink.

"No telling," Hollie's mom said. "I know that she's been acting a little different lately."

"How so?" he asked.

"Well, she seems sad. Maybe she's a bit anxious. I'm not sure. She doesn't talk much, and she was short-tempered when we took a walk through the old cemetery up the street last Saturday," she answered. "It's not like her to be testy with me."

"New school. New kids. She's under a lot of pressure," Hollie's dad said. "She snapped at me about going to bed last Friday night."

"And, she's getting to be *that* age!" Hollie's mom added.

"Yeah? Whatever that means!" Hollie had returned to the dining room. She began to laugh when she overheard what her mom said.

She also knew she had to try her best to win her case for what she was about to ask.

"Oh, you heard me," her mom said, feeling slightly guilty, but relieved that Hollie laughed.

"I always know what you guys are thinking anyway," Hollie said.

Hollie stood by the table, joining her parents, who had sat back down.

"What have you got there?" Hollie's dad asked.

Hollie ignored her dad's question, took a deep breath, closed her eyes for a few seconds, then looked directly at her mom and said, "I really did enjoy that walk with you in the cemetery, by the way."

Hollie's mom was speechless.

Hollie raised her eyebrows, smiled, and continued, "I'd like my friends Cherie and

Allie to come over here to spend the night next weekend so they can see where we've moved. I think they would like to see the house and experience the cemetery too."

Hollie's parents were not surprised by Hollie's request. They were surprised by the sudden hint of urgency. They didn't know what to say at first. Then Hollie's dad said, "So Hollie, do you have something to show us? What's that in your hand?"

Hollie carefully placed the two sets of homework side-by-side on the table. One paper was neat, and the other was untidy with a circled red letter F at the top of the page.

Hollie's parents, caught by surprise, silently stared at the papers and waited for Hollie to say something.

"I have to get the homework with the F signed and turn it back into the teacher tomorrow," Hollie said, uncertain of their

71

reaction. Then she blurted out, "It's hard, mom and dad. I'm trying. I'd ask for help, but I think you guys are always too tired and busy to help me. I've never had trouble in school before this year."

Hollie shook her head side-to-side but couldn't control what happened next. For the second time in the day, tears rolled down her cheeks.

"You both know I've never gotten an F in school before," Hollie sobbed.

Hollie's parents looked at each other with sad expressions in their eyes. They both immediately stood up and hugged Hollie together.

Cookies, who'd been sitting on the floor, walked over and rubbed against their legs. She wanted to be included in the group.

Soon Hollie calmed down.

Hollie and her parents came to an agreement. She must try harder to improve her homework grades and ask for help when she needed it. She wouldn't watch TV until her parents came home from work. They would all watch TV together after dinner if she didn't have questions about her homework.

If she didn't understand her homework, Hollie could sit outside on the deck and take a break from her lesson. Afterward, she could give it another try. Finally, if it seemed impossible, she could take a nap with Cookies or stay busy reading until her parents got home. One parent would always help her with her homework.

And, the last part of the agreement was the best part. Cherie and Allie could come to Niceville if their parents permit them and agree to drive them from Panama City. But, they could only stay one night.

An hour later, Hollie and her parents were all in bed.

KNOCK, KNOCK, KNOCK

THUD

"What was that?" Hollie's dad jumped out of bed and turned on the light in his bedroom.

"It sounded like something in the attic," Hollie's mom said.

KNOCK, KNOCK, KNOCK

THUD

KNOCK, KNOCK, KNOCK

THUD

"It sounds like it's on the roof," he said. "Maybe I should go see if anything is going on outside."

"I'll go with you," Hollie's mom said.

Hollie and Cookies, both awake, had heard the noise too. Hollie stayed in bed, afraid of another mysterious happening at night in her bedroom.

When she heard her parent's bedroom door open, Hollie didn't have time to say anything to them before they were both out the living room front door. Hollie jumped from her bed and peeked out her window blind. Both of her parents were standing in the front yard. They were looking upward in the tree, toward the roof of the house, turning their heads, searching in all directions. Hollie turned on the ceiling light in her room and waited for them to come back into the house.

"I heard it too," she told them when they came back inside.

"I thought maybe somebody was outside, doing something up by the road. We didn't see anything," Hollie's dad said, shaking his head, confused. "I have no idea what's going on."

"It was definitely loud enough!" Hollie's mom said.

KNOCK, KNOCK, KNOCK

THUD

Hollie and her parents looked at each other in wide-eyed silence, as if to ask each other *what is that noise?*

Cookies' fur was fluffed out, and her tail was thumping on the floor.

KNOCK, KNOCK, KNOCK

THUD

"Where the heck is that noise coming from?" her dad said in a controlled but obviously concerned voice. He peeked outside Hollie's window blinds.

"It almost sounds like it's coming from inside the walls, over in that corner," Hollie's mom said, pointing at the wall next to Hollie's bedroom closet.

They all sat down on Hollie's bed and waited.

KNOCK, KNOCK, KNOCK, THUD, didn't stop.

Finally, Hollie's dad said, "It has to be the limbs from that big tree in the front yard. Some of them are touching the roof. It's time for lights out. We've all got to get up in the morning to go to work and school."

He looked at Hollie and saw the worried look on her face. "You can leave your door open, Hollie," he said. "If you get scared, wake us up. And you, Cookies, stay away from the linen closet door!"

Once in their bedroom, Hollie's dad said to her mother, "It wasn't windy out there. There has to be some explanation for that noise. It's probably related to whatever got Cookies so worked up at the closet door the other night. There's nothing we can do about it right now."

"I hope this noise doesn't keep us awake all night," Hollie's mom said.

"Just cover your head with a pillow," Hollie's dad said to her, trying to ease her concern.

Hollie was more afraid and worried than the night before. "There has to be a connection with the eyes and noises," Hollie whispered to Cookies as they lay in the dark room. "Haunted. Yes, this house is haunted."

Unfortunately for Hollie, the floating blue orbs reappeared.

Chapter 9
A NEW FRIEND

Hollie was a tired, nervous mess the following day.

She tried her best to keep her eyes closed all through the night, imagining the blue eyes on the wall watching her in bed and the red eyes outside trying to peer into her bedroom window. She prayed she wouldn't hear the noises again. She tossed and turned, half-asleep at times but mostly awake.

Cookies didn't sleep either. Hollie's restlessness kept her awake. She didn't even have the energy to jump off the bed when Hollie got up to get ready for school.

Hollie rested her elbows on the desk at school and cupped her chin with both hands to hold up her head.

"Are you alright?" the girl sitting at the desk across the aisle whispered loudly at Hollie.

It startled Hollie at first. Since the first day of school, no one had ever spoken to her directly except the teacher. A few times in the lunchroom, someone said, *excuse me* or *oops*, if they bumped into her. All the kids who were old friends stayed together in their groups, paying no attention to the new girl, Hollie.

Hollie sat up straight before replying to her classmate, "Oh, yes. Thank you."

"You look dragged out and tired like you didn't get any sleep. I have to tell you that I heard what Ms. Smith said to you when she returned your homework papers yesterday. I felt bad for you. You look like you got in trouble and cried all night. I know I would be in trouble if I had to get a bad grade signed by my parents."

Hollie said, "It wasn't so bad with my parents. It's just other stuff."

"Okay, class, let's get started," the teacher announced from her desk at the front of the room.

The girl quickly whispered to Hollie, "My name is Elizabeth. If you want to talk, you can sit with my friends and me, and eat lunch together in the cafeteria."

Hollie nodded *yes* with her head and gave Elizabeth a big smile that said *thank you*.

Suddenly Hollie didn't feel so lonely at her school.

She thought, "I hope she doesn't think that I am a wimp. I must look like a total mess. She thinks I'm worried about my grades, which of course, I am. But she doesn't know what's worrying me the most. She doesn't know the fears I have because I live in a haunted house. I know there's a ghost in the attic that comes out with blue eyes or red eyes, and now it's banging on the walls. How could I ever tell a stranger that I think that the house I live in is haunted? Maybe it's a ghost from the cemetery. She'll think that I'm crazy, and she'll never speak to me again. Worse, she might tell everyone else too."

It was hard for Hollie, with thoughts about the haunted house, to pay attention to Ms. Smith, who was writing on the board with her back to the class.

Hollie glanced over at Elizabeth, who was smiling at Hollie and pointing at Ms. Smith beneath her desk, signaling Hollie to pay attention.

When the lunch bell finally rang, all of the students in the class rushed to get in a line by the classroom door. Since the first day of school, Hollie had waited to get in line last. Elizabeth patiently stood at her desk waiting for Hollie.

"Come on," Elizabeth urged Hollie. "Let's go hurry to get in line. The more time we're in here means the less time we have to talk at the lunch table."

The two girls sat with Elizabeth's other friends. From listening to the other girls talk, Hollie learned that they had the same interests as her. They talked about TV shows, pets, parents, the teacher, and their brothers or sisters.

Everything felt splendid for the first time since Hollie lived in Niceville, which she sometimes referred to as *Meanville* whenever she talked on the telephone to her friends Cherie and Allie.

At the end of the school day, Hollie forgot how tired she was and almost forgot about the past three sleepless nights until the school bus stopped in front of the house on Boggy Bayou. The late October days were getting shorter. The sun was lower in the sky. Bright, orange streaks of light filtered through the limbs of the tall hickory tree in the front yard, revealing spider webs.

She recalled the conversation she had with her dad Friday night on the deck. The front yard tree was where they'd seen the red spider hanging in mid-air. Hollie avoided looking at the tree.

"I'm home, but it's not home to me. It's just a crazy house. I hope we don't have to live here forever." Hollie moaned. "I can't believe dad wanted to know if this house is for sale. After what happened last night, I hope he never talks to the man down the street who owns this house."

She slowly walked, dragging her feet, to the front door. She could see Cookies' head peeking through the closed bedroom window blinds.

"Good," Hollie thought. "Mom didn't open them today. I hate it when she opens them before we leave the house in the morning."

84

Cookies jumped from the window and raced down the hallway to wait for Hollie at the front door. She was standing, her nose pressed against the side window, when Hollie opened the door.

They marched into the kitchen together to make the usual snack before they spent the rest of the afternoon in the small office.

Standing at the counter, making her peanut butter and jelly sandwich, Hollie felt something brush against her legs. It felt like a soft feather. Thinking it was Cookies, she looked down to see Cookies lying on her side on the kitchen floor.

"What are you doing over there, Cookies?" she asked.

Cookies looked up when Hollie said her name. She answered Hollie with a tiny meow.

"Are you talking to me?" Hollie asked Cookies while her eyes scanned the kitchen and living room. "I know I felt something. I thought it was your fur brushing up against my legs. Maybe it was just a breeze. Did I leave the front door open?"

Hollie took a few steps away from the kitchen counter and stretched her neck to see if the front door was shut. It was.

"I just got home, and it's already starting. I hate being in this house," Hollie said angrily, trying to ignore her feelings. "Now I'm imagining that I felt something touch my legs. However, last night mom and dad heard those knocks and thuds. I, all of us, didn't imagine that. Dad said spraying would kill the bugs and other critters. I wonder if it will kill the noises too? I can't imagine a bug or a spider so big that it makes a noise that loud. Wait. Maybe it's a mouse. That would be your job, Cookies. You would have to find and capture the mouse. Was that what you were trying to do in the linen closet last Friday night? Is it just a mouse in the house?"

Cookies looked up at Hollie when she heard her name again, hoping she would get a treat today.

"Anyway, Cookies," Hollie continued as she made her way to the office carrying her snack, "I hope dad takes care of it before the sleepover. I think it would be nice to have a sleepover on Halloween, but I know Cherie and Allie wouldn't want to go trick-or-treating here in Niceville. I think I should ask them to come over the Saturday before Halloween."

Hollie quickly forgot the feeling that something had brushed against her legs. Her thoughts centered on her friends from Panama City spending the night. She was also excited about making a friend at school.

"Maybe I should ask Elizabeth to spend the night, too," Hollie thought to herself.

That night, at the dinner table, Hollie's parents were comforted to see Hollie in a happy mood. It put their minds at ease.

Hollie's mind was on other things when she fell asleep. She had a new friend in her school, and she was inviting old friends for a sleepover. There was no time to think about floating blue eyes, glittering red eyes, spiders, or a mouse in the closet.

Everyone, including Cookies, was exhausted after a long day at school and work and the restless night before. They were all sound asleep and never heard the KNOCK, KNOCK, KNOCK, THUDs all night.

Chapter 10
SPIDERS IN THE ATTIC

Ms. Magdalene saw Hollie's parents out into the front yard last night. She didn't think that they looked afraid, and she didn't want them to be. The last thing Ms. Magdalene wanted was for anyone in the family to be scared.

"We haven't much time to finish our preparations. We certainly need to be more careful about the noise we make. Let's try to be a little quieter, Bandit."

Ms. Magdalene spoke to her cat in a gentle but firm voice. "If you're a good kitty, I'll agree to let you get out of the attic for a break so you can hang out in the hickory tree tomorrow night. I don't want you to get caught, though. I saw Hollie's dad looking up at the tree last night, and he might do it again." Ms. Magdalene playfully smiled at Bandit and added, "You don't want to scare Hollie's cat Cookies, either, do you?"

Bandit turned his head up to Ms. Magdalene to show her he was listening. He loved his owner.

When Ms. Magdalene died and was taken to the old cemetery, he followed the funeral party. He stayed by her tombstone for days. He was loyal and didn't want to be left behind, alone at the house on Boggy Bayou. He soon became the neighborhood's cat, roaming from house to house. He always hoped he might find Ms. Magdalene at someone else's home.

Sidney, Ms. Magdalene's best friend and neighbor, made sure that the last request Ms. Magdalene had before she died was honored. When Bandit died, there was a joyful reunion when Sidney buried him in the old cemetery alongside Ms. Magdalene.

"I think you already have a perfect outfit for Halloween," Ms. Magdalene said to Bandit and patted him on the head.

Bandit, part Siamese-cat, had sky-blue eyes. The fur on his body was the color of milk chocolate, except for the black fur circling his blue eyes. He appeared to be always wearing a black Halloween mask on his face.

Bandit was excited that another cat was living in the house. He did not want to admit to Ms. Magdalene that he'd already been peeking at Cookies in Hollie's bedroom at night. He didn't want to scare Cookies or Hollie, but his natural cat curiosity was stronger than his self-control. He loved being back in the house where he grew up. He'd even taken a peek at Cookies during the day in the kitchen as she watched Hollie make a snack. Bandit couldn't wait until he could play with Cookies on Halloween night.

"Cookie is a black cat," Ms. Magdalene talked while she worked. "All people think black cats and Halloween go together. Those are the same people who think the witches and monsters come out on Halloween. You're going to be the best cat ever on Halloween. That mask frames your beautiful blue eyes, and you don't look scary. Your mask is real, not fake."

Ms. Magdalene stopped what she was doing and gave Bandit a look of warning, "By the way, you know that I know you've sneaked into Hollie's room at night. If you scare Hollie and Cookies, it could ruin my plan. I want Hollie to be happy on Halloween night when she sees me in my costume."

Ms. Magdalene giggled at the thought of seeing Hollie's face when she made her grand appearance in her costume.

"Now, let's get to work, Bandit!" Ms. Magdalene ordered. "And remember, we need to be quieter. We don't want to wake up the family."

She giggled again. Then she lightly knocked against the attic wall with her fist three times.

A grape-sized, red spider dropped by a thread from the ceiling rafter, spinning the thread so fast it almost hit the floor. Just before it slammed to the floor, Bandit rushed after the spider. He nudged it with his nose, making the spider spin the silky, thin thread just above the floor. The spider, pushed by Bandit's nose, spun a long, horizontal thread all the way to the other side of the room. When it reached the wall, it climbed up the wall to the ceiling. There it joined hundreds of other red spiders living in the attic rafters.

Each time the spider reached the wall, Bandit hit the wall with a thud. He was enjoying his part, helping to create a costume for Ms. Magdalene on Halloween.

The idea of wearing a costume on Halloween had not occurred to Ms. Magdalene until

Hollie moved into the house on Boggy Bayou. When she heard the sadness and hopelessness in the voice of the young girl walking through the cemetery with her mother, Ms. Magdalene knew she needed to help her.

She used to make her Halloween costumes from fabric. This Halloween, she was making it with nature's art. Her long-time love of visiting the attic to see her spiders make delicate, lacy patterns was going to fulfill a higher purpose. The silky threads were going to be the material for her costume.

She was making the wings of an angel. The durable, powder-white, silky threads were going to be woven together to create a piece of silk large enough to drape over her arms, spread open wide when she wore it. In the light of the moon, the wings would sparkle and shine.

Ms. Magdalene paused from her work and floated above the floor.

94

"Bandit, it's true that at first sight, I might look a little scary," she said, "Hollie might think I am a ghost. I don't want to look like a ghost. I'm going to be her guiding angel. This costume has to look like real angel wings."

Bandit's blue eyes blinked behind his natural mask. He'd been scolded by Ms. Magdalene about scaring Hollie and Cookies. He paid attention to every word she said, but he wasn't worried. He knew that Halloween was going to be a fantastic night.

Bandit patiently waited for Ms. Magdalene to knock on the wall so another spider would drop. He enjoyed chasing it to the wall with his nose.

"So here are the rules until Halloween night arrives," she said with owner authority. "You cannot be haunting them in Hollie's room or the kitchen again. Furthermore, stay away from the hickory tree in the front yard. Just think how scared Hollie would be to see two blinking, blue eyes hovering in the tree limbs when she came home from school. She might be too afraid to go outside for Halloween."

Bandit knew Cookies liked to sit in Hollie's bedroom window and peek through the blinds to watch all the creatures that played in the hickory tree. Cookies would be fascinated to see a pair of blinking, blue eyes in the tree. It seemed like a great idea for tomorrow.

Lost in his thoughts about planning to hang out in the hickory tree, Bandit didn't act quickly enough when Ms. Magdalene knocked on the wall. He carelessly allowed the fast-spinning, red spider to slam to the floor with a splat. Stunned by the hard hit on the floor, the spider sat motionlessly. Bandit looked up at Ms. Magdalene. Her eyes twinkled with white sparks. She smiled before she firmly stepped down on the floor to nudge the lifeless spider with her dainty foot.

"Now fly away," she sang, dancing on her tip-toes. "Join your family outside. They're flying all over the bay and bayou. Sparkle, light up the night, and enjoy the fun."

The dead spider's iridescent spots flashed. Suddenly its body turned into a bright, glittering orb. The newly created orb flew up from the floor with fresh, new wings to the top of the attic ceiling. It made several fast passes through the rafter beams before it swooshed outside through the attic vent. There it joined all the other orbs flying amongst the cobwebs in the shoreline reeds of Blue Water Bay.

Chapter 11
THE SLEEPOVER

Hollie was surprised when she awoke to see daylight in her room and narrow rays of sunshine filtering through her bedroom blinds.

She felt refreshed from a whole night of sleep. No hauntings woke her up in the middle of the night.

She was looking forward to going to school.

"Cookies," Hollie said to her cat, sleeping soundly, curled up by her side. "Wake up."

She nudged Cookies with her leg. "Tonight, I'm calling Cherie and Allie to ask them to spend the night on Saturday. Today at school I'm going to ask Elizabeth if she wants to spend the night this Saturday, too. I haven't asked mom and dad if Elizabeth can stay, but one more person won't make a difference. I hope everyone will be able to come over."

It seemed like forever to wait for lunchtime. Hollie was anxious to ask Elizabeth about spending the night. Hollie was feeling more excited about Elizabeth spending the night than Cherie and Allie.

"I don't think that my mom will let me," Elizabeth said when Hollie asked. Elizabeth shrugged her shoulders and raised her eyebrows before she said matter-of-factly, "My mom wants to meet someone's parents before she allows me to stay overnight at a friend's house. That's her rule."

Elizabeth chewed her food.

Hollie was disappointed but didn't give up. "How do I get your mom to meet mine?" Hollie asked.

"I know!" Elizabeth nearly shouted. "You can ask your mom if she could bring you to my house to go trick-or-treating with me, and some of my other friends, on Halloween. We all go together every year. This year, after we finish, I'm having a party at my house. We're going to play games and have snacks. It only lasts for an hour or two. My mom can meet your mom when she drops you off at my house."

Upon hearing the invitation, she couldn't contain her excitement.

"That would be awesome," she said, smiling a huge smile. "I'm sure my mom won't mind taking me to your house. She's wanted me to make some new friends in Niceville. All of my friends in Panama City live too far away. Thank you for asking me to come to the party. Do you think your mom would call my mom tonight and give her directions to your house?"

"Yes, I know she'll do that," Elizabeth said.

"Great," Hollie said, still excited. "I'll tell my mom, too. She works, but she'll be home after five. Maybe they can talk after dinner. My mom would like to meet some new people in Niceville, too."

The two new friends exchanged telephone numbers.

It had been the best day of her life since moving to Niceville. Hollie skipped to the front door when she got off the school bus and did not think for a moment about all the things she hated about the house on Boggy Bayou.

"Cookies!" Hollie shouted when she found her waiting, as usual, at the front door. "I'm so glad to see you. Guess what? Today has been the best day of sixth grade. The best day ever!"

Hollie dropped her book bag on the floor and picked up Cookies to hug her. "I've been invited to a Halloween party."

Hollie gently released Cookies to the floor. Cookies rushed in front of Hollie, who was heading to the kitchen faster than usual, to make her afternoon snack.

Hollie talked fast while she slapped peanut butter on a slice of bread.

"If Cherie and Allie can come over and spend the night, I need to make a list of things we can do. First, I'll tell them about the spooky things that have happened in this house. I'm sure that they won't believe me if I say it's haunted. I'm definitely taking them for a walk in the cemetery. We should take flashlights just in case it gets dark before we get back home. I'm sure mom will go with us. She likes talking about the dead people buried in the cemetery. We should also walk to the end of the dock with flashlights. There's a chance we'll see those twinkling red eyes, like the ones we saw the other night. When we're ready to go to bed, we'll take all the pillows and blankets and put them on the floor. We can use one blanket to build a tent over us. I'll tell them to peek out of the tent if they want to see the floating, blinking, blue eyes above the TV. I'll tell them to listen for the knock, knock, knock, thuds too."

Cookies listened attentively and patiently, waiting for Hollie to take her snack to the office.

"And you know what else, Cookies," Hollie said, thinking she forgot about something. She looked down at Cookies, whose tail was swishing and sweeping up dust on the kitchen floor. "I'm so glad I'm going to a Halloween party and won't be trick-or-treating in this neighborhood. I wouldn't want to walk past the cemetery on Halloween night."

Hollie shared all of the good news of the day with her mom and dad when they got home.

Her mom said, "I'm thrilled you've made a new friend. I think you should call Cherie and Allie now to see if they haven't made other plans for Saturday night. Then they can ask their mom and dad to call us later tonight, after dinner."

"Do you think their parents will let them come this far?" Hollie's dad wondered more than asked. "It is almost an hour away from Panama City."

"I'm not sure, but they know you and me. Their parents know that they'll be safe with us. I suspect they know Cherie and Allie probably miss Hollie a little bit, too. They probably miss Hollie as much as she has missed them." Hollie's mom winked at Hollie when she said this.

As Hollie had hoped, Cherie and Allie were allowed to spend the night on Saturday.

When they arrived together in one car, it was a jubilant, happy reunion with hugs and laughter. The three friends chattered away while settling into Hollie's bedroom. Hollie told them to get ready for surprises.

"There will be things like you've never imagined. They scared me at first, but I'm used to them now," Hollie bragged.

They explored the old house's glassed-in patio, office, kitchen, and deck with the big tree growing in the middle of it.

"Let's go take a quick walk up to the cemetery before dinner," Hollie's mom suggested, as Hollie had asked her to do. The sun was just beginning to set. The glorious colors in the late autumn sky and the cool air put them all in a good mood. Gusty breezes blew around them when they stopped at the beautiful pink marble tombstone where Ms. Magdalene and Bandit were buried.

"It almost feels like ghosts are flying around here, doesn't it?" Hollie's mom joked.

After dinner, when complete darkness settled over the house, the hauntings Hollie had warned Cherie and Allie about happened.

First, they walked to the end of the dock, where they saw many flying, glittering, red eyes. Frightened by not knowing what they were, the girls rushed back into the house.

Once they were safe in Hollie's room, Cherie and Allie suggested they should peek out of the blinds, something that Hollie would never dream of doing, especially at night. The three girls climbed to the window ledge to sit with Cookies. They saw blue eyes floating above an extended branch of the hickory tree. The eyes were moving, and they blinked at them.

The three girls muffled their screams and jumped into Hollie's bed, where they stayed huddled together under the covers with a flashlight all night. They were not the least interested in building a tent or waiting to see the blue eyes appear in Hollie's bedroom.

The KNOCK, KNOCK, KNOCK, THUD above their heads kept everyone awake all night.

They tried to stay calm. No one slept, not even Cookies, who growled often and slapped her tail on the floor.

Cherie and Allie left early the following day. They promised to remain friends with Hollie, but agreed on the drive back to Panama City, they would never, *ever*, spend the night at the house on Boggy Bayou again.

Having her friends with her didn't make Hollie feel brave. After the visit, Hollie was even more frightened.

Chapter 12
MS. MAGDALENE
PREPARES

Ms. Magdalene left the cemetery soon after Hollie and her friends returned to the house. First, she made several passes over the top of the house on Boggy Bayou to hover over the hickory tree growing through the deck in the backyard.

The front yard tree was beautiful, but the hickory tree in the backyard, with the deck built around it, was still her favorite. It brought happy memories of the nights that she watched her husband's shrimp boat, reflecting its colored lights, across the black water. It had the appearance of a shiny pane of window glass in the darkness.

After her husband died, the fascination with spiders that began when she was a young girl grew stronger. She spent hours during the day collecting spiders from the hundreds of azalea bushes planted in the front yard. Secretly, she pretended to be clipping flowers or trimming the bushes.

Her neighbor Sidney and her brother-in-law thought her obsession with being in her yard was normal. Her odd behavior didn't bother them. They only knew Ms. Magdalene as a sweet, kind soul.

Bandit and Ms. Magdalene entered the attic together. Ms. Magdalene's voice was soft when she spoke to Bandit. "We've got only one week left to finish our plan. My task is for Hollie to see this beautiful display on Halloween night. Not only will she be surprised, but she will feel joy in her heart."

Ms. Magdalene continued talking, more to herself than to Bandit.

"I don't want her to be afraid. I want her to feel what she cannot touch. I want her to look at the night sky and see something besides the stars that sparkle and shine.

"When she sees my angel wings, I want her to think about the heavens. I want to open her heart to the light that shines in the day when the stars are there but not visible to the human eye like they are in the night sky. I want her to feel what her eyes are looking for but cannot always see.

"On Halloween night, I will appear with silky, shiny wings looking as soft as moonlit skin, floating gracefully in the air. Hollie will not fear to be in this house, or be unhappy, anymore. Let's get to work, Bandit."

Ms. Magdalene hit the wall so hard that several red spiders dropped from the rafter. Bandit skidded across the ceiling floor, happy to be chasing them all at the same time.

111

Ms. Magdalene began to hum. "This is your temporary home, my dear Hollie. Don't worry about the home you left back in Panama City. You'll be happy in any home from now on. You'll make friends everywhere you go. Squint your eyes and find the light that shines in everyone and everywhere."

Bandit meowed to Ms. Magdalene, "Cookies, the curious cat, will be thrilled to have something to chase on Halloween night."

Ms. Magdalene responded to Bandit. "All Saints Day is a time to celebrate. It is the most important day of the year for you too, Bandit. You've found someone to lead to a life of joy."

Bandit purred.

"Spiders are fun to chase right now," he thought. "But, Halloween night will be the beginning of the fun for me and for Cookies."

Chapter 13
HALLOWEEN NIGHT

October 31st was the traditional day to trick-or-treat. Still, Halloween parties were usually held on a Saturday before or Saturday after. This year trick-or-treating and the Halloween parties were both on the same Saturday.

That week at school, everyone was excited about planning for Halloween. Even the teachers were decorating their classrooms.

By Saturday evening, all the pumpkins were carved into fancy faces to decorate the front porch of homes. Candles were lit and placed inside the pumpkin. Bowls of candy and other treats were ready to give out when someone came to the door in a costume and declared, *Trick-or-Treat.*

Children and adults thought what made Halloween fun was not only candy but the costumes. It was a time when they could pretend to be someone else for a night. Some people liked to wear a costume to frighten people, like ghosts, skeletons, witches, or monsters. Others wore a costume to show who they would want to be in real life, like an action hero or princess. Whatever the favorite costume, everyone was excited and telling their friends.

It was difficult for Hollie to think about anything else but Saturday.

Hollie knew she did not want to wear a costume to scare anyone. This year Hollie wanted to dress up like a cowgirl. She thought it would be an easy costume to put together, and she'd always liked cowgirl characters in the movies and on TV.

"Are you excited about tonight?" Hollie's mom asked while she helped her get ready.

"You know I am," Hollie replied. "This is going to be the first day of fun that I've had since we moved to Niceville." Hollie vigorously nodded her head yes, again and again.

"What about last Saturday night when Cherie and Allie were here? Didn't you have some fun with them?" her mom asked.

"I don't think either of them liked it here at all. Both were nervous the whole time after it got dark. Maybe you, dad, and I were used to the noises and strange lights," Hollie answered.

Hollie's mom had heard the noises in the attic again, too. She wondered what Hollie meant by strange lights. She thought it best not to talk about it on Halloween night.

Hollie's mom helped her comb her hair into two pigtails. At the end of each braid, she tied a wide ribbon into a red bow. They found an old, red, western cowboy hat that Hollie used to play dress-up with when she was much younger. The little red hat had always been one of her favorites. It was too small for her head now, but it looked suitable for Halloween. She wore a western-style, checkered shirt she found at the thrift store. Her mother quickly assembled a denim skirt on her sewing machine. She didn't have a petticoat to wear underneath the dress as the cowgirls wore, but it had plenty of ruffles to make it swing when Hollie swayed her hips.

"I sure wish I could have bought those cowgirl boots at the thrift store," Hollie said. "They would look so perfect with this outfit."

"Hollie, we agreed that you probably would never wear cowgirl boots ever again. Don't think about them. You'll be happy your feet are in comfortable walking shoes when you're out walking tonight," her mother said.

Hollie looked at herself in the mirror and doubted what she saw. "Do I look dressed up in a real costume?"

116

"You look great, Hollie. Your costume looks authentic. It's better than some I've seen in the stores. You look like a real cowgirl," her mom said, looking at Hollie with pride and loving eyes. "You didn't want to look scary, remember? Let's add a little make-up. I can put some freckles on your nose and lines above your eyelids to make longer eyelashes. We can put some big red circles on your cheeks too."

"You'll make me look like a doll." Hollie giggled but liked the idea.

"Yes, a cowgirl doll." Her mom laughed.

The evening with Elizabeth and her friends was fun, but the time went by fast.

A boy who lived across the street from Elizabeth went trick-or-treating and to the party with them. The girls made fun of him and his friend for wearing silly-looking costumes made from aluminum tin foil and boxes. They were supposed to be robots.

Hollie enjoyed being with new people from school and telling them about herself. She learned things about them too.

Her heart was bursting with happiness on the ride back to the house on Boggy Bayou with her mom and dad, who sat in the front seat of the car. Hollie sat in the back seat, thinking about all the things she could do with her new friends.

"It was nice to meet some new people in Niceville," Hollie's dad said. "The only people we've met other than the people at work are the neighbors."

"Oh, by the way," Hollie's mom said. "Our neighbor, Sidney, was standing outside in her front yard when we were leaving the house. She saw us going to the car and came to the fence to ask about you. I told her you were at a party. We talked for a few minutes to be polite. That's why we were a little late. I told Elizabeth's mom I'd pick you up at nine."

"There were still some people at Elizabeth's house when I left," Hollie said. "Elizabeth's mom didn't mind. She told me that she enjoyed meeting you, and she also said Elizabeth and I should get together more often."

"Oh, that's good news," Hollie's mom said and paused before she continued. "Sidney said this was the time of year when she missed her friend, Magdalene, who used to live in our house. When she said that name, I realized that was the name on the pink marble tombstone in the old cemetery."

Everyone in the car was quiet.

Finally, Hollie's mom said, "Sidney told me Halloween was their favorite time of year. They would dress up and have a party at Magdalene's house, waiting for the children in the neighborhood to come to the door. After the Halloween party, Magdalene would host more neighborhood parties on other holidays. She especially liked Christmas and New

Year's Eve." Hollie's mom hesitated. "Sidney asked me if I'd send you over to get some candy. She said she had only four trick-or-treaters tonight, and she has a big bowl of candy left."

"I guess I can go over there tomorrow if she wants to give away some of her candy," Hollie said quietly.

"She wanted to see you in your costume tonight. She said it wouldn't be too late for her to wait. She's usually up until ten o'clock. She'll know it's you at the door because I told her you would be coming. She said she wouldn't open the door this late otherwise."

Hollie's mom turned her head sideways to look at Hollie in the back seat. "You do look cute in that costume. Especially the pigtails with big, red bows and your red cowgirl hat!"

"Mom," Hollie groaned. "Do I really have to walk over there tonight?"

"It won't hurt you," her dad broke in for Hollie's mom. "I'll stand on the front porch and watch for you. She's an elderly lady. I think she would enjoy the costume, and it will make her happy to see you." Hollie's dad checked the rearview mirror to see Hollie's cute face frowning.

"It'll only take you five minutes," he said. "Hey, look, we're passing the cemetery now. You could be groaning about real ghosts if you had to hide from them. All you have to do is walk next door."

Hollie's mom and dad both chuckled, but Hollie didn't think what he said was funny. She was upset now.

"You know what I don't understand?" Hollie said. "When we walked in the cemetery, there were a lot of gravestones that have the words *Rest in Peace* written on them. If we walk through the cemetery, are we disturbing their peace? Do they hear us? Are they only sleeping? Do the dead wake up and then come back alive? Is that why people talk about ghosts? Mom told me not to worry about ghosts. She said they're not real."

Hollie's dad drove the car into their driveway and turned off the engine.

"That's a lot of questions at one time, Hollie. Here's my best answer. Cemeteries are resting places for the dead. Some people think of them as a sleeping place for the dead until heaven calls them. Now, go on. Grab your candy bag and run on over to Sidney's house. You don't have to stay long. I'll wait for you outside."

Chapter 14
A SAINT ENDS THE NIGHT

Hollie could hear the leaves on the lawn crunching with each step she took toward Sidney's house on this quiet night. The street light was on, and the moon was shining bright, but the night felt darker than usual. Hollie took careful steps up to the front porch of the neighbor's house.

The neighbor seemed stranger than the strange people she'd taken candy from all night trick-or-treating.

Hollie was worried and thought to herself as she walked, "Sidney was friends with the woman called Magdalene. The same woman buried in the cemetery used to live in this house!"

Hollie suddenly felt connected to all the scary noises and things she'd seen in the last two weeks. Maybe Magdalene *was* a real ghost haunting the house.

Hollie wasn't sure what to expect when she met Sidney.

Hollie tapped on Sidney's door with her hand.

"Oh my! You look so darling," Sidney squealed when she opened her door and saw Hollie. "I love your costume. I love all of it."

"Thank you, ma'am," Hollie said politely.

"I have to tell you that Halloween used to be my favorite time of year. The lady who used to live in your house was my best friend. Halloween was the first of all her holiday parties. We used to have a grand time at Magdalene's parties." Sidney paused. "Well, I know you don't want to hear all about my stories right now. Anytime you want to listen to my stories, come right on over. I want you to know that you're living in a house that was

124

full of love and fun when Magdalene lived there. I hope you'll have friends over and have fun in it too."

Unexpectedly Hollie felt comfortable with Sidney. Sidney's wrinkled face was old-looking, but her eyes were shining and friendly when she smiled at Hollie. Hollie felt like she had met another new friend.

"Take as much candy as you want, dear," Sidney said.

"Thank you very much," Hollie said. She grabbed a fist full of candy and dropped it into her bag.

"Oh, please. Take more," Sidney coaxed Hollie.

"I've got a lot of candy already. I went trick-or-treating tonight with a new friend in her neighborhood."

"Oh, that sounds wonderful. Did you have a fun time with your new friend?" Sidney asked.

Hollie completely forgot that she'd been nervous about going to Sidney's house. "Yes, I did. Thank you. Okay, one more hand full, and then I need to go. My dad is waiting for me outside."

Hollie grabbed another fistful of candy and said, "I'm sure I'll see you soon."

Sidney said, "Please visit me anytime. Goodnight, dear."

Sidney watched Hollie skip across her paved driveway to the gate in the fence that separated their front yards. She turned to close her front door just as Hollie reached the gate, but something stopped her. A strong gust of air blew past her face, and she heard a whoosh. She left the door open and stood in the doorway to enjoy the breeze.

Hollie felt the breeze and heard the noise too. She stopped at the gate to look back at Sidney's house, where she saw Sidney still standing at the front door.

Hollie and Sidney waved their hands at each other to repeat goodnight.

A stronger breeze and swooshing sound caused them both to look up at the same time. Their eyes fixed on the tall hickory tree in front of Hollie's bedroom.

High above the tallest branch at the top of the tree, a white cloud, shaped like the wings of an angel, appeared. The silky wings swayed side-to-side, then floated down through the limbs and leaves. Transparent-like threads sparkled. They seemed to disappear only to reappear in another part of the tree. It was beautiful.

The beauty hypnotized Hollie. It seemed other-worldly and unique, something meant just for her to see.

Sidney was overcome with joy as she watched the shape of angel wings floating through the leaves and branches of the old hickory tree in the front yard of Hollie's house. Sidney immediately thought back to the day when the house cleaners found the hundreds of jelly jars, thousands of spiders, and millions of cobwebs in Magdalene's attic.

"That looks just like something Magdalene would do," Sidney thought. "Only she would turn spider webs into angel wings. One day, I hope I can be a saint like her. I just know it's her. She's clearing the path for another traveler here on earth."

Soon the wings disappeared, like clouds always do, into a foggy mist.

After the vision, Sidney's and Hollie's eyes met again.

Hollie called out to her, "Wasn't that the most beautiful cloud you've ever seen? If I didn't know it was a cloud, I could almost believe that the spiders intentionally built one huge web to look like the shape of angel wings in the tree."

"Oh, honey, it was beautiful! It was absolutely fantastic!" Sidney called back to Hollie from the doorway of her house. "Now, don't you forget to come back to visit me. I can tell you so many good stories about the fun parties we had in Magdalene's house."

"Okay," Hollie answered and skipped to her front door, where her dad was waiting.

Hollie's dad asked, "What were you and Sidney looking at? Did I hear you say something about spider webs?"

"Yes, we saw a cloud floating among the cobwebs in the hickory tree. But I think it was a ghost," Hollie laughed.

"Well, Hollie, while you've been watching clouds that you say look like ghosts, I've been watching these bugs crawling around in the soft, wet dirt by the flower bed. They're some type of flying beetle. When they fly, they give off a red glow. I've seen lightning bugs glow a white light, but I've never seen anything like this before. "

Together they watched an inch-long brown beetle take off from the ground and fly into the hickory tree. Suddenly two glittering red eyes appeared in the branches.

"It's Halloween, right, dad? All kinds of strange things happen," Hollie said before she and her dad turned to go into the house.

Hollie and her dad turned and walked into the house. They didn't notice the two blue orbs that had swooped through Hollie's window.

Inside, they found Hollie's mother standing in the living room, holding her stomach, and laughing. She was watching Cookies race up and down the hallway, back and forth, from the linen closet to the living room.

"I have no idea what's gotten into her," Hollie's mom said, wiping away tears of laughter. "She hasn't stopped running since I walked into the house. It's almost like she's chasing something."

"I bet it's a pair of blue eyes," Hollie thought to herself. "And, even if I hear noises in the attic tonight, I'm not going to be afraid. I know it's nothing that can harm me. It's been the best Halloween ever."

Hollie knew Cookies also had the best Halloween ever.

Hollie kept the feeling in her heart forever. She would never feel sad and lonely again. She knew an open heart can always make new friends.

Questions for the Reader

1. What do you think worries Hollie the most? Fear of living in a haunted house, or having no friends?
2. Why can't Hollie talk to her parents about what troubles her?
3. Why do you think Elizabeth took the first step to speak to Hollie?
4. Do you think Hollie imagined all the things she saw?
5. Define the word *orb.*
6. In the first chapter we learn about the life of Ms. Magdalene before she died. What do you think happened, and what do you know about her now?
7. What do you think upset Hollie most when she visited the cemetery the first time with her mother?
8. Do you think the noises in the attic stopped after Halloween?
9. Why do you think Hollie felt a strong urge to return to the cemetery?
10. Do you think Ms. Magdalene was improper for collecting spiders to watch them make webs?

About the Author

This is the second book for the author, who has lived in Panama City, Florida since 1978. Living, and working, near the Gulf of Mexico and a love of cats influences her writing. She graduated from high school in Rochester, New York; earned a Bachelor of Science Degree in Journalism from the University of Florida; and a Master of Science Degree in Psychology from The Florida State University.

Also Read "The Lucky Two" & "Eve at Peace"

Please visit the website
https://theluckytwo.com

Made in the USA
Columbia, SC
04 April 2024